First Edition
1 3 5 7 9 10 8 6 4 2
This book is set in Caslon Antique.
Printed in Hong Kong
Library of Congress Cataloging-in-Publication Data on file.
ISBN-13: 978-0-7868-3919-3 · ISBN-10: 0-7868-3919-8
Reinforced binding
Visit www.hyperionbooksforchildren.com

For
Angelic Ruiz,
★ ★ ★
who I expect to be
president in
thirty-two years.
L.P.

FOR
GRACE,
who asked
the question
"Where are the
girls?"
K.D.

VOTE
GRACE

FOR
GRACE

GRACE
FOR PRESIDENT

by
Kelly
DiPucchio
★
pictures by
LeUyen
Pham

HYPERION BOOKS
FOR CHILDREN
New York

One Monday morning in September, Mrs. Barrington rolled out a big poster with all of the presidents' pictures on it. Grace Campbell could not believe her eyes.

Where are the GIRLS?

"That is a very good question!" said Mrs. Barrington.
"The truth is, our country has never had a woman president."

"NO girl president?
EVER?"
Grace asked.

"No, I'm afraid not,"
said Mrs. Barrington.

Grace sat at her desk
and stewed. No girls?
Who'd ever heard of
such a crazy thing?

Finally, she raised her hand.

"Yes, Grace?"

"I've been thinking it over, and I'd like to be PRESIDENT!"

Several students in the class laughed.

"Well, I think that's a star-spangled idea, Grace!"
said Mrs. Barrington. "In fact, we can have our own
election right here at Woodrow Wilson Elementary!"

The snickering in the room stopped. Grace smiled.
"Would anyone else like to run for president?"
Mrs. Barrington asked the class.

Nobody raised their hand.

Becoming president was going to be easy! Grace thought.

The next day, Mrs. Barrington made an announcement.

"In the name of DEMOCRACY,

I have invited Mr. Waller's class to join our election.

Their class has nominated

THOMAS COBB

to be their presidential candidate!"

Grace's heart sank.

Thomas was the school
spelling bee champion.
His experiments always took
a blue ribbon at the science fair.
And he was captain of the soccer team.

Becoming president wasn't going to be
so easy, after all, Grace thought.

The teachers put the names of all fifty states and the District of Columbia into a hat. Everyone except for Grace and Thomas got to choose a state.

"I'm Texas!" said Anthony.

"I'm New Hampshire!" said Rose.

"I'm Michigan," said Robbie. "What does the number 17 mean?"

"Each state is assigned a number of electoral votes. That number is determined by how many people live in that state," said Mrs. Barrington. "Each of you will be a representative for your state."

"Altogether, our country has 538 electoral votes," Mr. Waller explained. "On election day, the candidate who receives 270 electoral votes or more wins the election!"

"Why 270?" asked Rose.

"That's more than half of all the electoral votes," Mr. Waller said.

Becoming president REALLY wasn't going to be so easy, Grace thought.

Grace came up with a campaign slogan:

Thomas came up with his own campaign slogan:

MAKE HISTORY! VOTE GRACE CAMPBELL FOR PRESIDENT!

VOTE FOR THOMAS COBB THE BEST MAN FOR THE JOB!

Grace listened to what issues were important to the students, and she made a list of campaign promises:

Thomas made up his own list of promises:

Grace made campaign posters and buttons.
Thomas made posters and buttons, too.

Each week, the teachers set aside time for
the candidates to meet with their constituents.

Polls were taken. Voters were making their choices.

Grace continued to campaign.

VOTE FOR GRACE

GRACE !!!

A TIME FOR GRACENESS

GRACE FOR PRESIDENT

Grace Campbell The Right Person

At recess, she gave SPEECHES.

Grace Campbell The Right Person

Make HISTORY at Woodrow Elementary! Vote for GRACE this coming November special Presidential and help make a change

RACE
The GIRL
or the JOB

VOTE GRACE

GRACE !!!

GRACE
is the
ONE

GRACE is the ONE

During lunch, she handed out free CUPCAKES.

A TIME FOR GRACENESS

GRACE for PRES

VOTE FOR GRACE

GRACE for IDENT

GRACENESS

KE HISTORY!
VOTE
RACE
for
IDENT!

GRACE
FOR

VOTE GRACE

GRACE !!!

After school, she held RALLIES.

MEANWHILE,
Thomas wasn't worried.

He had cleverly calculated that the **BOYS**
held slightly more electoral votes than the **GIRLS**.

At recess, Thomas studied his spelling words.

During lunch, he worked on his latest science experiment.

After school, he played soccer.

Even before the election, Grace made good on her promises. She joined the safety squad. She organized a school beautification committee, and she volunteered her time in the school cafeteria.

In early November, Woodrow Wilson Elementary hosted
a special Election Day assembly. Grace and Thomas took
their places onstage as the school band began to play.

Henry was the first representative to approach the microphone.

The
Yellowhammer
State of Alabama
casts its 9
electoral votes
for Thomas Cobb!

Fletcher said,

The Last Frontier
State of Alaska casts
its 3 electoral
votes for the best
man for the job,
Thomas Cobb!

Hannah called out:

The Grand Canyon
State of Arizona
casts its 10
electoral votes for
Grace Campbell!

And so it went. State after state after state cast their electoral
votes. The scoreboard in the gymnasium kept track of the totals.

The voting demonstration was quickly coming to an end.
Clara approached the podium.

The Badger State of Wisconsin casts its 10 votes for my best friend, Grace Campbell!

Grace looked at the scoreboard.
Thomas had 268 electoral votes. She had 267.
There was only one state still unaccounted for.

Thomas grinned. Grace felt sick.
Sam walked up to the microphone.

He looked at Thomas.

He looked at Grace.
He looked down at Grace's handmade flag.

Sam didn't say a word.

"What are you waiting for?"
Thomas whispered.

The band stopped playing.

All eyes were on Wyoming.

Finally, Sam cleared his throat.

The gymnasium erupted in loud cheers
(and a few boos).
Mrs. Barrington approached the podium.
"With 270 electoral votes, the winner is Grace Campbell!"

Thomas looked stunned. Grace hugged Sam.
"Why did you do it?" she asked.
Sam handed Grace his flag. "Because," he said,
"I thought you were the best person for the job."

The following week, the students in Mrs. Barrington's class were preparing for their Career Day presentations.

Grace volunteered to go first. She stood at the front of the room and glanced at the poster still hanging on the wall.

My name is Grace Campbell, and when I grow up, I'm going to be president of the United States.

This time, everyone believed that she would.

★ AUTHOR'S NOTE ★

You might be wondering what the Electoral College is and how it works. You're not alone! Many adults have a hard time understanding the process. First of all, the Electoral College has nothing to do with going to college. It's our country's system for electing a president.

When people vote in presidential elections, what they're really doing is telling the representatives from their states who they'd like to become president of the United States. These elected representatives, known as the "electors," then cast their *electoral* votes for the candidate who received the most *popular* votes in his or her state. Currently there are 538 electors in the United States.

Each state is assigned a number of electoral votes equal to the number of senators and representatives it has. Every state has two senators, but the number of representatives each state has depends on its population. So, the more people a state has, the more electoral votes it has. California, for example, has a large population. It has two senators (just like the other states) and 53 members of the House of Representatives (unlike the other states). Simply put:

2 senators + 53 representatives = 55 electoral votes in the state of California

Likewise, states that are less populated will have fewer representatives and fewer electoral votes. In an election, the presidential candidate to win the majority of electoral votes—270—is the winner.

Why does our country use such a complicated system? The Electoral College was written into our Constitution all the way back in 1787. Americans didn't have televisions, radios, or computers back then. It was very difficult for average citizens to be accurately informed about all the candidates who were running for president. The Electoral College system gave elected officials a much bigger role in choosing the president of the United States. Even though most Americans do have access to more information today, a Constitutional amendment would have to be passed in order to change the current system. Hundreds of suggestions for changing the election process have been offered over the years, but so far, not one of them has been approved by Congress.

You might be wondering why regular people should even bother to vote in elections if it's the electoral votes from state representatives that determine which man or woman gets to be president. I'll tell you why! It's those individual votes from regular people that add up to become the *popular* vote in each state. Electors cast all of their electoral votes for the candidates their constituents have given the majority of votes to. So every single vote really is very important!

−K.D.